BE ABLE

HIMANI SHARMA

be happy

Contents

CHAPTER ONE

Life

Life is a characteristic that distinguishes physical entities that have biological processes, such as signaling and self-sustaining processes, from those that do not, either because such functions have ceased (they have died) or because they never had such functions and are classified as inanimate. Various forms of life exist, such as plants, animals, fungi, protists, archaea, and bacteria. Biology is the science that studies life.

There is currently no consensus regarding the definition of life. One popular definition is that organisms are open systems that maintain homeostasis, are composed of cells, have a life cycle, undergo metabolism, can grow, adapt to their environment, respond to stimuli, reproduce and evolve. Other definitions sometimes include non-cellular life forms such as viruses and viroids.

Abiogenesis is the natural process of life arising from non-living matter, such as simple organic compounds. The prevailing scientific hypothesis is that the transition from non-living to living entities was not a single event, but a gradual process of increasing complexity. Life on Earth first appeared as early as 4.28 billion years ago, soon after ocean formation 4.41 billion years ago, and not long after the formation of Earth 4.54 billion years ago.[1][2][3][4] The earliest known life forms are bacteria.[5][6] Life on Earth is probably descended from an RNA world,[7] although RNA-based life may not have been the first life to have existed.[8][9] Metal-Binding Proteins that allowed biological electron transfer may have evolved from minerals.[10] The classic 1952 Miller–Urey experiment and similar research demonstrated that most amino acids, the chemical constituents of the proteins used in all living organisms, can be synthesized from inorganic compounds under conditions intended to replicate those of the early Earth. Complex organic molecules occur in the Solar System and in interstellar space, and these molecules may have provided starting material for the development of life on Earth.[11][12][13][14]

Since its primordial beginnings, life on Earth has changed its environment on a geologic time scale, but it has also adapted to survive in most ecosystems and conditions. Some microorganisms, called extremophiles, thrive in physically or geochemically extreme environments that are detrimental to most other life on Earth. The cell is considered the structural and functional unit of life.[15][16] There are two kinds of cells, prokaryotic and eukaryotic, both of which consist of cytoplasm enclosed within a membrane and contain many biomolecules such as proteins and nucleic acids. Cells reproduce through a process of cell division, in which the parent cell divides into two or more daughter cells.

In the past, there have been many attempts to define what is meant by "life" through obsolete concepts such as Odic force, hylomorphism, spontaneous generation and vitalism, that have now been disproved by biological discoveries. Aristotle is considered to be the first person to classify organisms. Later, Carl Linnaeus introduced his system of binomial nomenclature for the classification of species. Eventually new groups and categories of life were discovered, such as cells and microorganisms, forcing significant revisions of the structure of relationships between living organisms. Though currently only known on Earth, life need not be restricted to it, and many scientists speculate in the existence of extraterrestrial life. Artificial life is a computer simulation or human-made reconstruction of any aspect of life, which is often used to examine systems related to natural life.

Death is the permanent termination of all biological processes which sustain an organism, and as such, is the end of its life. Extinction is the term describing the dying-out of a group or taxon, usually a species. Fossils are the preserved remains or traces of organisms.

Contents

Definitions

The definition of life has long been a challenge for scientists and philosophers.[17][18][19] This is partially because life is a process, not a substance.[20][21][22] This is complicated by a lack of knowledge of the characteristics of living entities, if any, that may have developed outside of Earth.[23][24] Philosophical definitions of life have also been put forward, with similar difficulties on how to distinguish living things from the non-living.[25] Legal definitions of life have also been described and debated, though these generally focus on the decision to declare a human dead, and the legal ramifications of this decision.[26] As many as 123 definitions of life have been compiled.[27] One definition seems to be favored by NASA: "a self-sustaining chemical system capable of Darwinian evolution".[28][29][30][31] More simply, life is, "matter that can reproduce itself and evolve as survival dictates".[32][33][34]

Biology

See also: Organism

The characteristics of life

Since there is no unequivocal definition of life, most current definitions in biology are descriptive. Life is considered a characteristic of something that preserves, furthers or reinforces its existence in the given environment. This characteristic exhibits all or most of the following traits:[19][35][36][37][38][39][40]

Homeostasis: regulation of the internal environment to maintain a constant state; for example, sweating to reduce temperature

Organization: being structurally composed of one or more cells – the basic units of life

Metabolism: transformation of energy by converting chemicals and energy into cellular components (anabolism) and decomposing organic matter (catabolism). Living things require energy to maintain internal organization (homeostasis) and to produce the other phenomena associated with life.

Growth: maintenance of a higher rate of anabolism than catabolism. A growing organism increases in size in all of its parts, rather than simply accumulating matter.

Adaptation: the ability to change over time in response to the environment. This ability is fundamental to the process of evolution and is determined by the organism's heredity, diet, and external factors.

Response to stimuli: a response can take many forms, from the contraction of a unicellular organism to external chemicals, to complex reactions involving all the senses of multicellular organisms. A response is often expressed by motion; for example, the leaves of a plant turning toward the sun (phototropism), and chemotaxis.

Reproduction: the ability to produce new individual organisms, either asexually from a single parent organism or sexually from two parent organisms.

These complex processes, called physiological functions, have underlying physical and chemical bases, as well as signaling and control mechanisms that are essential to maintaining life.

Alternative definitions

See also: Entropy and life

From a physics perspective, living beings are thermodynamic systems with an organized molecular structure that can reproduce itself and evolve as survival dictates.[41][42] Thermodynamically, life has been described as an open system which makes use of gradients in its surroundings to create imperfect copies of itself.[43] Another way of putting this is to define life as "a self-sustained chemical system capable of undergoing Darwinian evolution", a definition adopted by a NASA committee attempting to define life for the purposes of exobiology, based on a suggestion by Carl Sagan.[44][45][46] A major strength of this definition is that it distinguishes life by the evolutionary process rather than its chemical composition.[47]

Others take a systemic viewpoint that does not necessarily depend on molecular chemistry. One systemic definition of life is that living things are self-organizing and autopoietic (self-producing). Variations of this definition include Stuart Kauffman's definition as an autonomous agent or a multi-agent system capable of reproducing itself or themselves, and of completing at least one thermodynamic work cycle.[48] This definition is extended by the apparition of novel functions over time.[49]

Viruses

Main articles: Virus and Virus classification

Adenovirus as seen under an electron microscope

Whether or not viruses should be considered as alive is controversial. They are most often considered as just gene coding replicators rather than forms of life.[50] They have been described as "organisms at the edge of life"[51] because they possess genes, evolve by natural selection,[52][53] and replicate by making multiple copies of themselves through self-assembly. However, viruses do not metabolize and they require a host cell to make new products. Virus self-assembly within host cells has implications for the study of the origin of life, as it may support the hypothesis that life could have started as self-assembling organic molecules.[54][55][56]

Biophysics

Main article: Biophysics

To reflect the minimum phenomena required, other biological definitions of life have been proposed,[57] with many of these being based upon chemical systems. Biophysicists have commented that living things function on negative entropy.[58][59] In other words, living processes can be viewed as a delay of the spontaneous diffusion or dispersion of the internal energy of biological molecules towards more potential microstates.[17] In more detail, according to physicists such as John Bernal, Erwin Schrödinger, Eugene Wigner, and John Avery, life is a member of the class of phenomena that are open or continuous systems able to decrease their internal entropy at the expense of substances or free energy taken in from the environment and subsequently rejected in a degraded form.[60][61] The emergence and increasing popularity of biomimetics or biomimicry (the design and production of materials, structures, and systems that are modeled on biological entities and processes) will likely redefine the boundary between natural and artificial life.[62]

Living systems theories

Living systems are open self-organizing living things that interact with their environment. These systems are maintained by flows of information, energy, and matter.

Definition of cellular life according to Budisa, Kubyshkin and Schmidt.

Budisa, Kubyshkin and Schmidt defined cellular life as an organizational unit resting on four pillars/cornerstones: (i) energy, (ii) metabolism, (iii) information and (iv) form. This system is able to regulate and control metabolism and energy supply and contains at least one subsystem that functions as an information carrier (genetic information). Cells as self-sustaining units are parts of different populations that are involved in the unidirectional and irreversible open-ended process known as evolution.[63]

Some scientists have proposed in the last few decades that a general living systems theory is required to explain the nature of life.[64] Such a general theory would arise out of the ecological and biological sciences and attempt to map general principles for how all living systems work. Instead of examining phenomena by attempting to break things down into components, a general living systems theory explores phenomena in terms of dynamic patterns of the relationships of organisms with their environment.[65]

Gaia hypothesis

Main article: Gaia hypothesis

The idea that Earth is alive is found in philosophy and religion, but the first scientific discussion of it was by the Scottish scientist James Hutton. In 1785, he stated that Earth was a superorganism and that its proper study should be physiology. Hutton is considered the father of geology, but his idea of a living Earth was forgotten in the intense reductionism of the 19th century.[66]:10 The Gaia hypothesis, proposed in the 1960s by scientist James Lovelock,[67][68] suggests that life on Earth functions as a single organism that defines and maintains environmental conditions necessary for its survival.[66] This hypothesis served as one of the foundations of the modern Earth system science.

Nonfractionability

Robert Rosen devoted a large part of his career, from 1958[69] onwards, to developing a comprehensive theory of life as a self-organizing complex system, "closed to efficient causation"[70] He defined a system component as "a unit of organization; a part with a function, i.e., a definite relation between part and whole." He identified the "nonfractionability of components in an organism" as the fundamental difference between living systems and "biological machines." He summarized his views in his book Life Itself.[71] Similar ideas may be found in the book Living Systems[72] by James Grier Miller.

Life as a property of ecosystems

A systems view of life treats environmental fluxes and biological fluxes together as a "reciprocity of influence,"[73] and a reciprocal relation with environment is arguably as important for understanding life as it is for understanding ecosystems. As Harold J. Morowitz (1992) explains it, life is a property of an ecological system rather than a single organism or species.[74] He argues that an ecosystemic definition of life is preferable to a strictly biochemical or physical one. Robert Ulanowicz (2009) highlights mutualism as the key to understand the systemic, order-generating behavior of life and ecosystems.[75]

Complex systems biology

Main article: Complex systems biology

See also: Mathematical biology

Complex systems biology (CSB) is a field of science that studies the emergence of complexity in functional organisms from the viewpoint of dynamic systems theory.[76] The latter is also often called systems biology and aims to understand the most fundamental aspects of life. A closely related approach to CSB and systems biology called relational biology is concerned mainly with understanding life processes in terms of the most important relations, and categories of such relations among the essential functional components of organisms; for multicellular organisms, this has been defined as "categorical biology", or a model representation of organisms as a category theory of biological relations, as well as an algebraic topology of the functional organization of living organisms in terms of their dynamic, complex networks of metabolic, genetic, and epigenetic processes and signaling pathways.[77][78] Alternative but closely related approaches focus on the interdependence of constraints, where constraints can be either molecular, such as enzymes, or macroscopic, such as the geometry of a bone or of the vascular system.[79]

Darwinian dynamic

Main article: Evolutionary dynamics

CHAPTER TWO

Operator theory

The structure of the souls of plants, animals, and humans, according to Aristotle

Hylomorphism is a theory first expressed by the Greek philosopher Aristotle (322 BC). The application of hylomorphism to biology was important to Aristotle, and biology is extensively covered in his extant writings. In this view, everything in the material universe has both matter and form, and the form of a living thing is its soul (Greek psyche, Latin anima). There are three kinds of souls: the vegetative soul of plants, which causes them to grow and decay and nourish themselves, but does not cause motion and sensation; the animal soul, which causes animals to move and feel; and the rational soul, which is the source of consciousness and reasoning, which (Aristotle believed) is found only in man.[95] Each higher soul has all of the attributes of the lower ones. Aristotle believed that while matter can exist without form, form cannot exist without matter, and that therefore the soul cannot exist without the body.[96]

This account is consistent with teleological explanations of life, which account for phenomena in terms of purpose or goal-directedness. Thus, the whiteness of the polar bear's coat is explained by its purpose of camouflage. The direction of causality (from the future to the past) is in contradiction with the scientific evidence for natural selection, which explains the consequence in terms of a prior cause. Biological features are explained not by looking at future optimal results, but by looking at the past evolutionary history of a species, which led to the natural selection of the features in question.[97]

Spontaneous generation

Main article: Spontaneous generation

Spontaneous generation was the belief that living organisms can form without descent from similar organisms. Typically, the idea was that certain forms such as fleas could arise from inanimate matter such as dust or the supposed seasonal generation of mice and insects from mud or garbage.[98]

The theory of spontaneous generation was proposed by Aristotle,[99] who compiled and expanded the work of prior natural philosophers and the various ancient explanations of the appearance of organisms; it was considered the best explanation for two millennia. It was decisively dispelled by the experiments of Louis Pasteur in 1859, who expanded upon the investigations of predecessors such as Francesco Redi.[100][101] Disproof of the traditional ideas of spontaneous generation is no longer controversial among biologists.[102][103][104]

Vitalism

Main article: Vitalism

Vitalism is the belief that the life-principle is non-material. This originated with Georg Ernst Stahl (17th century), and remained popular until the middle of the 19th century. It appealed to philosophers such as Henri Bergson, Friedrich Nietzsche, and Wilhelm Dilthey,[105] anatomists like Xavier Bichat, and chemists like Justus von

Liebig.[106] Vitalism included the idea that there was a fundamental difference between organic and inorganic material, and the belief that organic material can only be derived from living things. This was disproved in 1828, when Friedrich Wöhler prepared urea from inorganic materials.[107] This Wöhler synthesis is considered the starting point of modern organic chemistry. It is of historical significance because for the first time an organic compound was produced in inorganic reactions.[106]

During the 1850s, Hermann von Helmholtz, anticipated by Julius Robert von Mayer, demonstrated that no energy is lost in muscle movement, suggesting that there were no "vital forces" necessary to move a muscle.[108] These results led to the abandonment of scientific interest in vitalistic theories, especially after Buchner's demonstration that alcoholic fermentation could occur in cell-free extracts of yeast.[109] Nonetheless, the belief still exists in pseudoscientific theories such as homeopathy, which interprets diseases and sickness as caused by disturbances in a hypothetical vital force or life force.[110]

Origin

Life timeline

This box:

view

talk

edit

−4500 —

–

—

–

−4000 —

–

—

–

–3500 —

–

—

–

–3000 —

–

—

–

–2500 —

–

—

–

–2000 —

–

—

–

–1500 —

–

—

–

–1000 —

–

—

–

–500 —

–

—

–

0 —

Water
Single-celled life
Photosynthesis

Eukaryotes
Multicellular life
P
l
a
n
t
s

Arthropods Molluscs
Flowers
Dinosaurs
Mammals
Birds
Primates
H
a
d
e
a
n

A
r
c
h
e
a
n

P
r
o
t
e
r
o
z
o
i
c

P
h
a
n
e
r
o
z
o
i
c

←

Earth formed

←

Earliest water

←

Earliest known life

←

LHB meteorites

←

Earliest oxygen

←

Pongola glaciation*

←

Atmospheric oxygen

←

Huronian glaciation*

←

Sexual reproduction

←

Earliest multicellular life

←

Earliest fungi

←

Earliest plants

←

Earliest animals

←

Cryogenian ice age*

←

Ediacaran biota

←

Cambrian explosion

←

Andean glaciation*

←

Earliest tetrapods

←

Karoo ice age*

←

Earliest apes / humans

←

Quaternary ice age*
(million years ago)
*Ice Ages
Main article: Abiogenesis
The age of Earth is about 4.54 billion years.[111][112][113] Evidence suggests that life on Earth has existed for at least 3.5 billion years,[114][115][116][117][118][119][120][121][122] with the oldest physical traces of life dating back 3.7 billion years;[123][124][125] however, some hypotheses, such as Late Heavy Bombardment, suggest that life on Earth may have started even earlier, as early as 4.1–4.4 billion years ago,[114][115][116][117][118] and the chemistry leading to life may have begun shortly after the Big Bang, 13.8 billion years ago, during an epoch when the universe was only 10–17 million years old.[126][127][128]

More than 99% of all species of life forms, amounting to over five billion species,[129] that ever lived on Earth are estimated to be extinct.[130][131]

Although the number of Earth's catalogued species of lifeforms is between 1.2 million and 2 million,[132][133] the total number of species in the planet is uncertain. Estimates range from 8 million to 100 million,[132][133] with a more narrow range between 10 and 14 million,[132] but it may be as high as 1 trillion (with only one-thousandth of one percent of the species described) according to studies realized in May 2016.[134][135] The total number of related DNA base pairs on Earth is estimated at 5.0 x 1037 and weighs 50 billion tonnes.[136]

In comparison, the total mass of the biosphere has been estimated to be as much as 4 TtC (trillion tons of carbon).[137] In July 2016, scientists reported identifying a set of 355 genes from the Last Universal Common Ancestor (LUCA) of all organisms living on Earth.[138]

All known life forms share fundamental molecular mechanisms, reflecting their common descent; based on these observations, hypotheses on the origin of life attempt to find a mechanism explaining the formation of a universal common ancestor, from simple organic molecules via pre-cellular life to protocells and metabolism. Models have been divided into "genes-first" and "metabolism-first" categories, but a recent trend is the emergence of hybrid models that combine both categories.[139]

There is no current scientific consensus as to how life originated. However, most accepted scientific models build on the Miller–Urey experiment and the work of Sidney Fox, which show that conditions on the primitive Earth favored chemical reactions that synthesize amino acids and other organic compounds from inorganic precursors,[140] and phospholipids spontaneously form lipid bilayers, the basic structure of a cell membrane.

Living organisms synthesize proteins, which are polymers of amino acids using instructions encoded by deoxyribonucleic acid (DNA). Protein synthesis entails intermediary ribonucleic acid (RNA) polymers. One possibility for how life began is that genes originated first, followed by proteins;[141] the alternative being that proteins came first and then genes.[142]

However, because genes and proteins are both required to produce the other, the problem of considering which came first is like that of the chicken or the egg. Most scientists have adopted the hypothesis that because of this, it is unlikely that genes and proteins arose independently.[143]

Therefore, a possibility, first suggested by Francis Crick,[144] is that the first life was based on RNA,[143] which has the DNA-like properties of information storage and the catalytic properties of some proteins. This is called the RNA world hypothesis, and it is supported by the observation that many of the most critical components of cells (those that evolve the slowest) are composed mostly or entirely of RNA. Also, many critical cofactors (ATP, Acetyl-CoA, NADH, etc.) are either nucleotides or substances clearly related to them. The catalytic properties of RNA had not yet been demonstrated when the hypothesis was first proposed,[145] but they were confirmed by Thomas Cech in 1986.[146]

One issue with the RNA world hypothesis is that synthesis of RNA from simple inorganic precursors is more difficult than for other organic molecules. One reason for this is that RNA precursors are very stable and react with each other very slowly under ambient conditions, and it has also been proposed that living organisms consisted of other molecules before RNA.[147] However, the successful synthesis of certain RNA molecules under the conditions that existed prior to life on Earth has been achieved by adding alternative precursors in a specified order with the precursor phosphate present throughout the reaction.[148] This study makes the RNA world hypothesis more plausible.[149]

Geological findings in 2013 showed that reactive phosphorus species (like phosphite) were in abundance in the ocean before 3.5 Ga, and that Schreibersite easily reacts with aqueous glycerol to generate phosphite and glycerol 3-phosphate.[150] It is hypothesized that Schreibersitecontaining meteorites from the Late Heavy Bombardment could have provided early reduced phosphorus, which could react with prebiotic organic molecules to form phosphorylated biomolecules, like RNA.[150]

In 2009, experiments demonstrated Darwinian evolution of a two-component system of RNA enzymes (ribozymes) in vitro.[151] The work was performed in the laboratory of Gerald Joyce, who stated "This is the first example, outside of biology, of evolutionary adaptation in a molecular genetic system."[152]

Prebiotic compounds may have originated extraterrestrially. NASA findings in 2011, based on studies with meteorites found on Earth, suggest DNA and RNA components (adenine, guanine and related organic molecules) may be formed in outer space.[153][154][155][156]

In March 2015, NASA scientists reported that, for the first time, complex DNA and RNA organic compounds of life, including uracil, cytosine and thymine, have been formed in the laboratory under outer space conditions, using starting chemicals, such as pyrimidine, found in meteorites. Pyrimidine, like polycyclic aromatic hydrocarbons (PAHs), the most carbon-rich chemical found in the universe, may have been formed in red giants or in interstellar dust and gas clouds, according to the scientists.[157]

According to the panspermia hypothesis, microscopic life—distributed by meteoroids, asteroids and other small Solar System bodies—may exist throughout the universe.[158][159]

Environmental conditions

Cyanobacteria dramatically changed the composition of life forms on Earth by leading to the near-extinction of oxygen-intolerant organisms.

The diversity of life on Earth is a result of the dynamic interplay between genetic opportunity, metabolic capability, environmental challenges,[160] and symbiosis.[161][162][163] For most of its existence, Earth's habitable environment has been dominated by microorganisms and subjected to their metabolism and evolution. As a consequence of these microbial activities, the physical-chemical environment on Earth has been changing on a geologic time scale, thereby affecting the path of evolution of subsequent life.[160] For example, the release of molecular oxygen by cyanobacteria as a by-product of photosynthesis induced global changes in the Earth's environment. Because oxygen was toxic to most life on Earth at the time, this posed novel evolutionary challenge

CHAPTER THREE

The inert component

The inert components of an ecosystem are the physical and chemical factors necessary for life—energy (sunlight or chemical energy), water, heat, atmosphere, gravity, nutrients, and ultraviolet solar radiation protection.[181] In most ecosystems, the conditions vary during the day and from one season to the next. To live in most ecosystems, then, organisms must be able to survive a range of conditions, called the "range of tolerance."[182] Outside that are the "zones of physiological stress," where the survival and reproduction are possible but not optimal. Beyond these zones are the "zones of intolerance," where survival and reproduction of that organism is unlikely or impossible. Organisms that have a wide range of tolerance are more widely distributed than organisms with a narrow range of tolerance.[182]

Extremophiles

Further information: Extremophile

To survive, selected microorganisms can assume forms that enable them to withstand freezing, complete desiccation, starvation, high levels of radiation exposure, and other physical or chemical challenges. These microorganisms may survive exposure to such conditions for weeks, months, years, or even centuries.[160]

Extremophiles are microbial life forms that thrive outside the ranges where life is commonly found.[183] They excel at exploiting uncommon sources of energy. While all organisms are composed of nearly identical molecules, evolution has enabled such microbes to cope with this wide range of physical and chemical conditions. Characterization of the structure and metabolic diversity of microbial communities in such extreme environments is ongoing.[184]

Microbial life forms thrive even in the Mariana Trench, the deepest spot in the Earth's oceans.[172][173] Microbes also thrive inside rocks up to 1,900 feet (580 m) below the sea floor under 8,500 feet (2,600 m) of ocean.[172][174] Expeditions of the International Ocean Discovery Program found unicellular life in 120°C sediment that is 1.2 km below seafloor in the Nankai Trough subduction zone.[185]

Investigation of the tenacity and versatility of life on Earth,[183] as well as an understanding of the molecular systems that some organisms utilize to survive such extremes, is important for the search for life beyond Earth.[160] For example, lichen could survive for a month in a simulated Martian environment.[186][187]

Chemical elements

All life forms require certain core chemical elements needed for biochemical functioning. These include carbon, hydrogen, nitrogen, oxygen, phosphorus, and sulfur—the elemental macronutrients for all organisms[188]—often represented by the acronym CHNOPS. Together these make up nucleic acids, proteins and lipids, the bulk of living matter. Five of these six elements comprise the chemical components of DNA, the exception being sulfur. The latter is a component of the amino acids cysteine and methionine.

The most biologically abundant of these elements is carbon, which has the desirable attribute of forming multiple, stable covalent bonds. This allows carbon-based (organic) molecules to form an immense variety of chemical arrangements.[189] Alternative hypothetical types of biochemistry have been proposed that eliminate one or more of these elements, swap out an element for one not on the list, or change required chiralities or other chemical properties.[190][191]

DNA

Main article: DNA

Deoxyribonucleic acid is a molecule that carries most of the genetic instructions used in the growth, development, functioning and reproduction of all known living organisms and many viruses. DNA and RNA are nucleic acids; alongside proteins and complex carbohydrates, they are one of the three major types of macromolecule that are essential for all known forms of life. Most DNA molecules consist of two biopolymer strands coiled around each other to form a double helix. The two DNA strands are known as polynucleotides since they are composed of simpler units called nucleotides.[192] Each nucleotide is composed of a nitrogen-containing nucleobase—either cytosine (C), guanine (G), adenine (A), or thymine (T)—as well as a sugar called deoxyribose and a phosphate group. The nucleotides are joined to one another in a chain by covalent bonds between the sugar of one nucleotide and the phosphate of the next, resulting in an alternating sugar-phosphate backbone. According to base pairing rules (A with T, and C with G), hydrogen bonds bind the nitrogenous bases of the two separate polynucleotide strands to make double-stranded DNA. The total amount of related DNA base pairs on Earth is estimated at 5.0×10^{37}, and weighs 50 billion tonnes.[136] In comparison, the total mass of the biosphere has been estimated to be as much as 4 TtC (trillion tons of carbon).[137]

DNA stores biological information. The DNA backbone is resistant to cleavage, and both strands of the double-stranded structure store the same biological information. Biological information is replicated as the two strands are separated. A significant portion of DNA (more than 98% for humans) is non-coding, meaning that these sections do not serve as patterns for protein sequences.

The two strands of DNA run in opposite directions to each other and are therefore anti-parallel. Attached to each sugar is one of four types of nucleobases (informally, bases). It is the sequence of these four nucleobases along the backbone that encodes biological information. Under the genetic code, RNA strands are translated to specify the sequence of amino acids within proteins. These RNA strands are initially created using DNA strands as a template in a process called transcription.

Within cells, DNA is organized into long structures called chromosomes. During cell division these chromosomes are duplicated in the process of DNA replication, providing each cell its own complete set of chromosomes. Eukaryotic organisms (animals, plants, fungi, and protists) store most of their DNA inside the cell nucleus and some of their DNA in organelles, such as mitochondria or chloroplasts.[193] In contrast, prokaryotes (bacteria and archaea) store their DNA only in the cytoplasm. Within the chromosomes, chromatin proteins such as histones compact and organize DNA. These compact structures guide the interactions between DNA and other proteins, helping control which parts of the DNA are transcribed.

DNA was first isolated by Friedrich Miescher in 1869.[194] Its molecular structure was identified by James Watson and Francis Crick in 1953, whose model-building efforts were guided by X-ray diffraction data acquired by Rosalind Franklin.[195]

Classification

Main article: Biological classification

The hierarchy of biological classification's eight major taxonomic ranks. Life is divided into domains, which are subdivided into further groups. Intermediate minor rankings are not shown.

Antiquity

The first known attempt to classify organisms was conducted by the Greek philosopher Aristotle (384–322 BC), who classified all living organisms known at that time as either a plant or an animal, based mainly on their ability to move. He also distinguished animals with blood from animals without blood (or at least without red blood), which can be compared with the concepts of vertebrates and invertebrates respectively, and divided the blooded animals into five groups: viviparous quadrupeds (mammals), oviparous quadrupeds (reptiles and amphibians), birds, fishes and whales. The bloodless animals were also divided into five groups: cephalopods, crustaceans, insects (which included the spiders, scorpions, and centipedes, in addition to what we define as insects today), shelled animals (such as most molluscs and echinoderms), and "zoophytes" (animals that resemble plants). Though Aristotle's work in zoology was not without errors, it was the grandest biological synthesis of the time and remained the ultimate authority for many centuries after his death.[196]

Linnaean

The exploration of the Americas revealed large numbers of new plants and animals that needed descriptions and classification. In the latter part of the 16th century and the beginning of the 17th, careful study of animals commenced and was gradually extended until it formed a sufficient body of knowledge to serve as an anatomical basis for classification.

In the late 1740s, Carl Linnaeus introduced his system of binomial nomenclature for the classification of species. Linnaeus attempted to improve the composition and reduce the length of the previously used many-worded names by abolishing unnecessary rhetoric, introducing new descriptive terms and precisely defining their meaning.[197] The Linnaean classification has eight levels: domains, kingdoms, phyla, class, order, family, genus, and species.

The fungi were originally treated as plants. For a short period Linnaeus had classified them in the taxon Vermes in Animalia, but later placed them back in Plantae. Copeland classified the Fungi in his Protoctista, thus partially avoiding the problem but acknowledging their special status.[198] The problem was eventually solved by Whittaker, when he gave them their own kingdom in his five-kingdom system. Evolutionary history shows that the fungi are more closely related to animals than to plants.[199]

As new discoveries enabled detailed study of cells and microorganisms, new groups of life were revealed, and the fields of cell biology and microbiology were created. These new organisms were originally described separately in protozoa as animals and protophyta/thallophyta as plants, but were united by Haeckel in the kingdom Protista; later, the prokaryotes were split off in the kingdom Monera, which would eventually be divided into two separate groups, the Bacteria and the Archaea. This led to the six-kingdom system and eventually to the current three-domain system, which is based on evolutionary relationships.[200] However, the classification of eukaryotes, especially of protists, is still controversial.[201]

As microbiology, molecular biology and virology developed, non-cellular reproducing agents were discovered, such as viruses and viroids. Whether these are considered alive has been a matter of debate; viruses lack characteristics of life such as cell membranes, metabolism and the ability to grow or respond to their environments. Viruses can still be classed into "species" based on their biology and genetics, but many aspects of such a classification remain controversial.[202]

In May 2016, scientists reported that 1 trillion species are estimated to be on Earth currently with only one-thousandth of one percent described.[134]

The original Linnaean system has been modified over time as follows: